The World According to Moominmamma

First published 2023 by Macmillan Children's Books

an imprint of Pan Macmillan

The Smithson, 6 Briset Street, London EC1M 5NR

EU representative: Macmillan Publishers Ireland Limited

1st Floor, The Liffey Trust Centre, 117–126 Sheriff Street Upper, Dublin 1, D01 YC43

Associated companies throughout the world www.panmacmillan.com

ISBN: 978-1-5290-7386-7

Text and illustrations © Moomin Characters™

1 3 5 7 9 8 6 4 2

A CIP catalogue record for this book is available from the British Library.

Printed in China

MIX

Paper | Supporting
responsible forestry

FSC® C116313

The World According to Moominmamma

Macmillan Children's Books

Meet Moominmamma

Moominmamma is calm and collected, kind and loving, brave and adventurous.

If anyone is sad or anxious, Moominmamma will do her best to help and console – and she knows her family will do the same for her when she needs them.

She makes sure that the Moominhouse is a safe and welcoming place, both for her family and for visitors. Whenever visitors come to the Moominhouse, Moominmamma wants to know when their birthdays are. The one celebrating their birthday gets to choose dessert!

Moominmamma is never seen without her striped apron and trusty handbag, which is full of important things, such as dry socks, sweets, stomach powder and string.

It's thanks to Moominmamma that everything runs so smoothly in the Moomin household. She finds solutions to even the most difficult dilemmas and tries to see the silver lining in every cloud. But she needs time to herself too – painting, gardening, collecting shells or making bark boats. There is much more to her than just being a 'traditional' mother; she is creative, artistic and fearless – and always ready for an adventure.

Mothers are . . .

Loving

"Mother,
I love you terribly,"

said Moomintroll.

All of Moominmamma was
round in the way that mamas
should be round.

Moomintroll feels extremely glum.

He wants his home, his bed, his mum.

"Mamma will know what to do!"

Flower after flower appeared on the
wall, roses, marigolds, pansies, peonies . . .
No one was more surprised than
Moominmamma herself. She had no
idea she could paint so well.

"Well, it'll be another nice long day
tomorrow," said Moominmamma.
"And it's all yours from beginning to
end. Now isn't that a lovely thought!"

Mothers are . . .

Kind

"All nice things
are good for you."

- Moominmamma

"I don't want friends who are kind without really liking me and I don't want anybody who is kind just so as not to be unpleasant. And I don't want anybody who is scared. I want somebody who is never scared and who really likes me. I want a mamma!"

— Toft

"Welcome home, Moomin, safe and sound,

And welcome, friends! Come, gather round!

Time for a feast," *said Mamma.* "Drink!

Scrumptious delights all round, I think.

A shell, a rose, a fresh baked bun?

Oh, I'm so glad to see my son!"

"Now have a good sleep, Ninny.
Sleep as late as you can. There'll be
tea for you in the morning any time you
want. And if you happen to get a funny
feeling or if you want anything, just
come downstairs and tinkle."

- Moominmamma

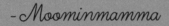

Mothers are . . .

Strong

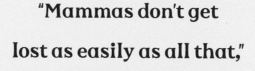

"Mammas don't get

lost as easily as all that,"

said Little My.

"You can always

find them in a corner

somewhere if you only look."

She did not feel worried, and that was a good thing. They had decided never to be worried about each other, so that they could each keep a good conscience and have as much freedom as possible. So Moominmamma started some new knitting without making any fuss, and somewhere to the west Moominpappa was wandering along with a dim idea firmly in his head.

At first Moominmamma was frightened too,
but then she said soothingly: "It's really a very
little creature. Wait, and I'll shine a light on it.
Everything looks worse in the dark, you know."

All at once an ant-lion came

strolling across the sand.

He looked very cross and said:

"This is my beach! You must go away!"

"We certainly shan't,"

said Moominmamma.

"So there!"

No one was quite as
stubborn as Moominmamma.
He wondered whether she would
get her apple tree after all.
She deserved to.

Mothers are . . .

Adventurous

"Today I feel like doing something unusual," said Moominmamma . . . "One gets so tired of always sitting in the same place."

"But you mustn't frighten us like that,"
said Moominpappa.
"You must remember that we're used to your
being here when we come home in the evening."

"That's just it,"
Moominmamma sighed.
"But one needs a change sometimes. We take
everything too much for granted, including
each other. Isn't that true, dearest?"

"There's a lot of things one can't understand,"

Moominmamma said to herself.

"But why should everything be exactly

as one is used to having it?"

"I'll dive now, Mamma,"

said Moomintroll.

"Tell him not to, please,"

said the Snorkmaiden anxiously.

"Well, why should I?"

replied his mother.

"If he thinks it's thrilling."

The Story of the Moomins

Moominmamma and her family and friends live in
Moominvalley, a place inspired by Tove Jansson's summers
spent on the islands off Finland and Sweden. The
Moomins, along with carefree Snufkin, fearless Little My,
timid Sniff and loyal Snorkmaiden, have many adventures
on land and in water, and encounter much danger – but
always return safely to the Moominhouse.

Tove Jansson was born in Finland in 1914. She drew her
first Moomin as a teenager, and the first Moomin story,
The Moomins and the Great Flood, was published in 1945.
She created a total of thirteen Moomin books, which have
been translated into 56 languages. The Moomins are
now famous and beloved all around the world and have
appeared in a hugely successful comic strip, television
series, plays, films, and even opera and ballet adaptations.

References

Page 12   Moominland Midwinter

Page 13   Moominvalley in November

Page 14   The Book About Moomin,

                 Mymble and Little My

Page 15   Comet in Moominland

Page 16   Moominpappa at Sea

Page 17   Moominpappa at Sea

Page 20   The Exploits of Moominpappa

Page 21   Moominvalley in November

Page 22   The Book About Moomin,

                 Mymble and Little My

Page 25   Tales from Moominvalley

Page 28   Moominpappa at Sea

Page 29   Tales from Moominvalley

Page 30   The Moomins and the Great Flood

Page 31   The Moomins and the Great Flood

Page 33   Moominpappa at Sea

Page 36   Finn Family Moomintroll

Page 38   Moominpappa at Sea

Page 39   Moominsummer Madness

Page 40   Moominsummer Madness